Dear Parent:
Your child's love of reading starts here!

Every child learns to read in a different w   ed.
You can help your young reader improve
by encouraging his or her own interests c   de
your child's spiritual development by reading stories with biblical values
and Bible stories, like I Can Read! books published by Zonderkidz. From
books your child reads with you to the first books he or she reads alone,
there are I Can Read! books for every stage of reading:

SHARED READING
Basic language, word repetition, and whimsical
illustrations, ideal for sharing with your emergent reader.

BEGINNING READING
Short sentences, familiar words, and simple concepts for
children eager to read on their own.

READING WITH HELP
Engaging stories, longer sentences, and language play
for developing readers.

READING ALONE
Complex plots, challenging vocabulary, and high-interest
topics for the independent reader.

ADVANCED READING
Short paragraphs, chapters, and exciting themes for the
perfect bridge to chapter books.

I Can Read! books have introduced children to the joy of reading since
1957. Featuring award-winning authors and illustrators and a fabulous
cast of beloved characters, I Can Read! books set the standard for
beginning readers.

A lifetime of discovery begins with the magical words "I Can Read!"

Visit www.icanread.com for information on enriching your child's reading experience.
Visit www.zonderkidz.com for more Zonderkidz I Can Read! titles.

"... Your father in heaven is not willing that any of these little ones should perish."
—*Matthew 18:14*

ZONDERKIDZ

The Berenstain Bears® and the Little Lost Cub
Copyright © 2011 by Berenstain Publishing, Inc.
Illustrations © 2011 by Berenstain Publishing, Inc.

Requests for information should be addressed to:
Zonderkidz, *Grand Rapids, Michigan 49530*

Library of Congress Cataloging-in-Publication Data

Berenstain, Jan, 1923 –
    The Berenstain Bears and the little lost cub / written by Jan and Mike Berenstain.
       p.   cm. – (I can read. Level 1)
    ISBN 978-0310-72100-0 (softcover)
    [1. Lost children—Fiction. 2. Bears—Fiction. 3. Christian life—Fiction. I. Berenstain,
  Michael. II. Title.
    PZ7. B44826Ben 2011
    [E]–dc22   2010016476

All Scripture quotations, unless otherwise indicated, are taken from the Holy Bible, *New International Version*®, *NIV*®. Copyright © 1973, 1978, 1984, 2011 by Biblica, Inc.™ Used by permission. All rights reserved worldwide.

Any Internet addresses (websites, blogs, etc.) and telephone numbers printed in this book are offered as a resource. They are not intended in any way to be or imply an endorsement by Zondervan, nor does Zondervan vouch for the content of these sites and numbers for the life of this book.

Editor: Mary Hassinger
Art direction & design: Kris Nelson

Printed in China

11 12 13 14 15 16 /SCC/ 10 9 8 7 6 5 4 3 2 1

ZONDERkidz

I Can Read!

BEGINNING READING 1

The Berenstain Bears
and the
Little Lost Cub

Story and Pictures By
Jan and Mike Berenstain

Living Lights™

GOOD DEED SCOUTS

ZONDERVAN.com/
AUTHORTRACKER
follow your favorite authors

The Good Deed Scouts were walking

down Main Street in Bear Town.

They were looking for a good deed to do.

"What's that I hear?" wondered Scout Lizzy.

"Someone is crying,"
said Scout Fred.
They went around a corner.
They found a little cub
crying his eyes out.

"What's wrong?" asked Scout Brother.

"I can't find my mom!" sobbed the cub.

"I'm lost!"

"Don't worry," said Scout Sister.

"We will take care of you."

"As the Bible says," pointed out Fred,
"'I will search for the lost and bring
back the strays.'"
"Good point, Fred," said Brother.

"The first thing to do," said Lizzy, "is find a police bear."

"There's Chief Bruno now," said Sister.

"Excuse us, Chief," Sister said. "This little cub is lost."

"Good work, Scouts!" said the Chief.

"I will take him to the police station.

Come with us. Maybe you can help."

"Oh, boy!" said the Scouts.

"The police station!"

At the station, Chief Bruno
gave the lost cub a lollipop.
"We will see if his mother calls
to say he is lost," said the Chief.

"But that might take a while," said Brother. "The poor little cub wants his mom now."

14

"I know what!" said Lizzy.

"One of us can stay here

to keep the lost cub company.

The others can take pictures of him

around town.

Maybe we can find his mother."

"Good idea!" said Chief Bruno.

Chief Bruno took a picture of the cub.

He made copies.

Brother, Sister, and Fred took the pictures.

They walked around Bear Town.

Lizzy stayed with the lost cub.

The Good Deed Scouts went everywhere
with pictures of the lost cub.
They went to the playground.

They went to the shopping center.

They went to the Town Square.

The Good Deed Scouts did not give up.

They went to the movie theater.

They went to the bus stop.

They went to the train station.

Just like the shepherd in the Bible

looking for his one lost sheep,

the Scouts did not give up.

The lost cub was having a nice time

at the police station.

He had an ice-cream cone.

He played checkers with Lizzy.

"King me!" he said.

The Good Deed Scouts were back
where they started.
They showed pictures of the
cub to everyone.

"A lady was just here

looking for a lost cub," someone said.

"Where did she go?" asked Fred.

"To the police station," said another.

The Good Deed Scouts ran all the way

to the police station.

At the police station,

the lost cub's mother was hugging him.

"Oh, my little lost cub!" she cried.

"I was so worried!"

"Mama!" cried the little cub.

"My own little Orville!" said his mother.

"Orville!?"

said the Scouts.

"How can I thank you enough?"
said the lost cub's mother
to the Good Deed Scouts.
"Well, ma'am,…" said Brother.

"I'll just have to give you each
a big kiss!" she said.
"But..." the Scouts said.
And the lost cub's
mother gave them
each a big kiss.

"The Good Deed Scouts to the rescue!"

laughed Chief Bruno.